Little Girl Lost But Found

Written & illustrated by Catherine Harris
Copyright © Catherine Harris
Copyright © April 3, 2023

Little Girl Lost But Found | Meredith Etc

Publisher:
Meredith McGee DBA Meredith Etc

Meredith Etc
1052 Maria Court
Jackson, MS 39204
www.meredithetc.com

Blog: meredithetc.com
facebook Meredith Etc
Meredithetc

All rights reserved.

Printed in the U.S.A.

Printed and bound by Kindle Publishing
7"x10" black and white interior
1,402 words
34 pages

Little Girl Lost But Found | Meredith Etc

Once again, the nighttime made its fall.
Baby girl needed to see the entire room.

Her back was pressed against the wall.
Her mind was overloaded with fear.

She held her blanket so tight.
She kept it so close.
Always near and always dear

Many nights she asked mama, "Can I sleep with you?"
Mama replied, "I can do better than that. I'm going to empower
you!"

Scared little girl,
lean on me.
I've been up & down this road.

Once upon a time the scared little girl was me.
Some things in life were very, very scary.
Some things in life were very, very sweet.
Sometimes it made me cranky.
Sometimes it made me want to be by myself & all alone.
No TV, no telephone, only music to drown the pain.

Sitting at a window,
watching the clouds,
watching some rain,
sometimes I cried.
Family didn't notice.
Family didn't see.
But a great thing happened.

Like a bird going south for winter,
the fear flew far, far, far.

Far away from me,
like a shooting star,
gliding through the night sky,
no longer in hiding,
and I was ready to go on that ride.

I started the work.
I started my fight.
I grew strong.
In my heart and in my mind,
one foot at a time.

Climbing along the mountain side of life,
I decided to be happy - you see.

I am happy & unafraid.
That is the life I chose for me.

And you my dear can have the same.
You will capture strong thoughts.
Negative thoughts you will learn to tame.

Every day I wake up,
He gives out brand new mercy.
I rise to fight, fight, fight,
fight everyday with all my might,
but not with my fists.

This fight was of a different kind.
Something different was taking place on the inside.
When the sun disappeared
& the moon said, "Hi,"
darkness was all around.

Once again it became nighttime.

My mind is made up.
I refuse to be sad & afraid.
I said I will go to bed happy,
with a big smile on my face.
I get up in the morning,
and face life again.
I will not let fear get the best of me.

I put my mind on God.
I kept my mind on Him.

I practice positive thinking day after day.
I found myself.
I found the way.
Becoming happier was a lot of work.
It was like having a job.
I keep going,
and I do not stop.

Because of faith,
every time you bet, I will win,
sometimes I got tired,
but I would not give in.
Now, I win every time.

When things are bad & when things are good
He gave me peace.

Like nothing else in this world ever, ever, could
I heard a wise man say, "God has not given us a spirit of fear."

He's given us power, love & a sound mind.
That was what I needed to hear.
The scary things people did & brought my way,
lost its power,
lost its grip.
I refused to go backwards.
I refused to slip.

I said to myself,
I will hold my head up high,
I will no longer wonder why, why, why.
When the nighttime comes,
I will not let fear beat me up,
or drain me dry.

I will lie down in peace,
relax and snuggle under the covers,
and calmly close my eyes.

My body will rest.
My faith will get its exercise.

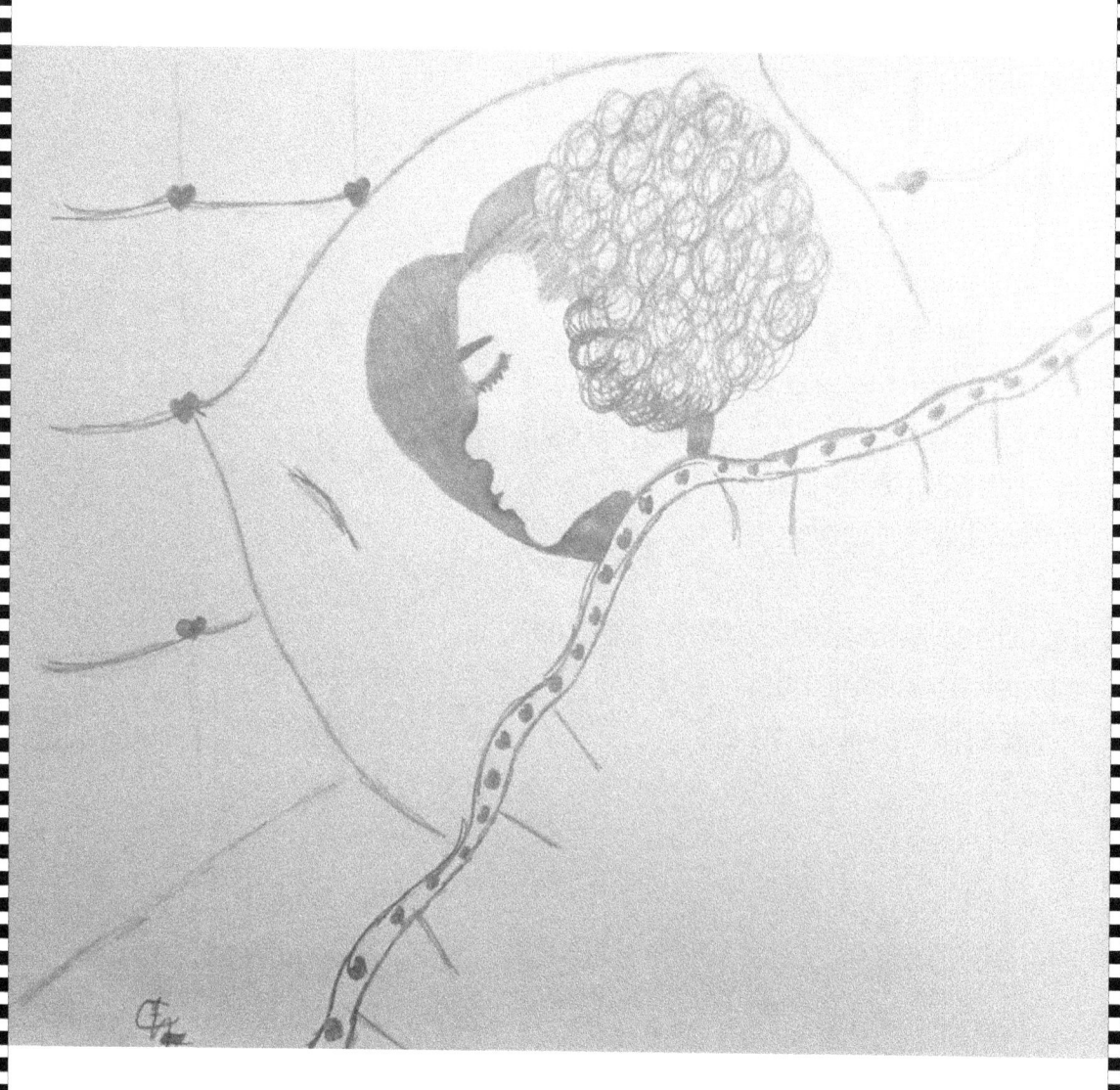

Bad things might still happen.
Bad things might still appear.
I made up my mind to pray,
And when I do, He hears.

A broken & contrite spirit,
He will not turn away.
In that moment He listens,
to what you & I have to say.

I cast my cares upon Him,
because He cares for me.
Every day I wake up,
He gives out brand new mercy.
His strength is perfect,
when I am weak.

I choose to have a great attitude.
I trust these words.
I will still have peace.

There is compassion for me.
There is compassion for you.

So, I held onto this,
and when it came time to snooze,
like a favorite doll, blanket, or bear,
I was comforted.

Those are the words I rely on.
Those are the words I use,
to shake off fear,
past the stars,
and even past the moon,
deep into the night,
and all through the sky.

I was comforted & protected.
The angels are always on standby.

If fear came, I did not shrink.
Like the captain of a ship,
sailing the ocean and the sea,
when the weather is calm,
when the weather is stormy,
the Lord is my light and my salvation.

Whom shall I Fear?
I push away doubts.
I put on a smile.
I stand at the helm.
And I continue to steer.
Full steam ahead, I go.

Through beautiful waters,
I watch as the waves crash,
I watch the waves as they flow.
I see amazing dolphins jump out of the water and spin.
I make it to my destination.

I am thankful,
filled with peace,
and I cannot wait to sail again.

I can do all things through Christ,
who strengthens me.

Whether or not the sun is shining
I still love the beach.
Sand on my toes,
with my favorite ice cream.

Whether or not I hear loud thunder,
whether or not I see a shadow,
sounds like a voice in the night are calling me,
even if it is Pitch Black,
with scary clouds,
and the skies won't quit storming.
Guess what?

I will always imagine me,
with a brand-new helmet,
driving a shiny race car with stripes.

I'm zooming a long fast.
I'm zooming along free.
It feels great.
It feels amazing.

My eyes are on nature,
thanking God for making the trees.

If He is for me,
who can be against me?

It no longer matters.
It's no longer a thing.

He does exceedingly abundantly,
above all that I could ever ask,
or think.

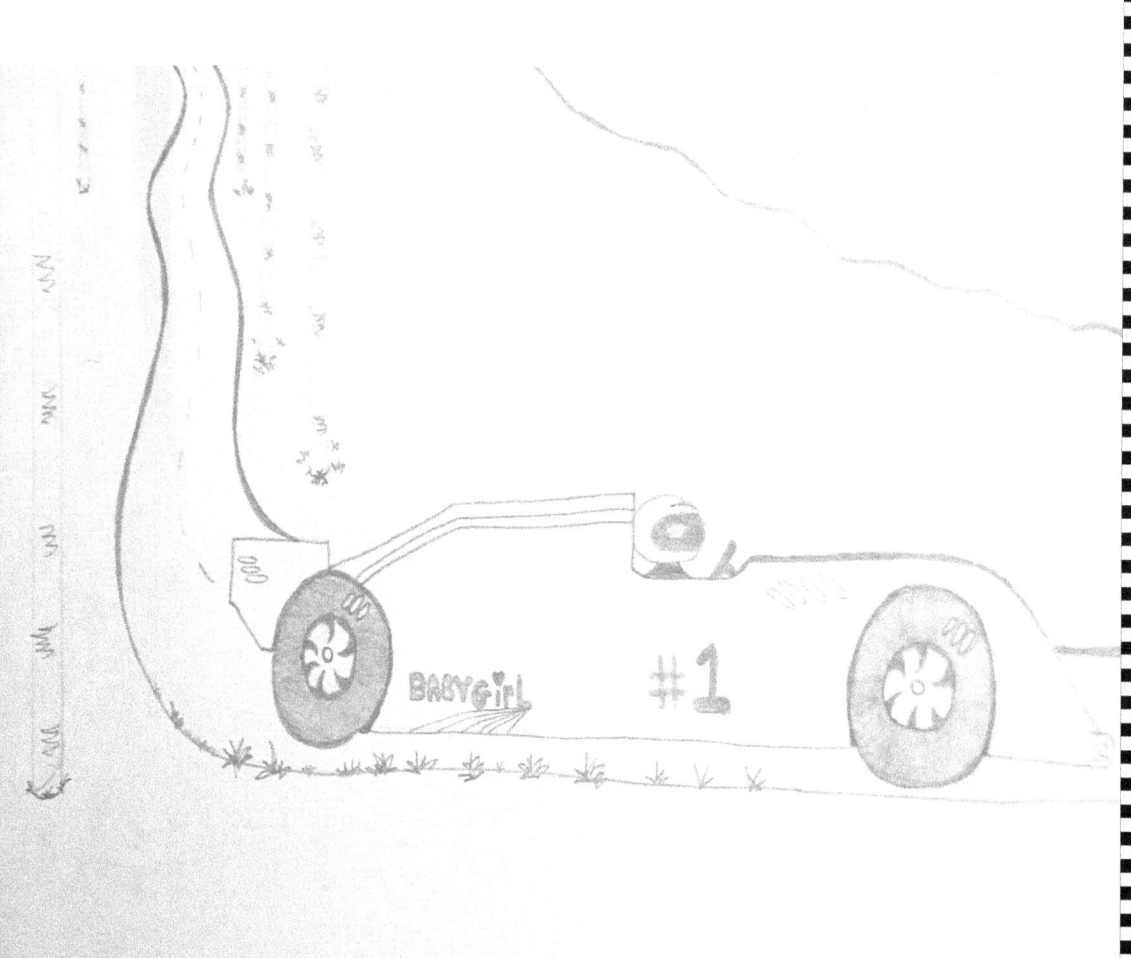

I remind myself of this…
all through the day.

If I get scared,
if I am disappointed,
this is what I remind myself,
this is what I say.

I encourage myself.
This is how I push through.
I refuse to stay down,
and neither should you.

It's a lot of work.
And it can be done.
Walking by faith,
is how to fight the battle.
This is how you get it done.

I believed, I believed, I believed,
with all my heart,
because I chose to believe.

I started living the part,
of a happy kid,
who loved sunshine, sparkles & pink.

I controlled my thoughts.
If fear came,
I just couldn't shrink.
I cast down bad imaginations.
I concentrated on faith, hope & love,
strength & going forward.

These are the thoughts to focus on
when you are in battle.

This is how you must think.

You are more than a conqueror.
The battle starts in our minds.
Now, I give you the keys.
Seek my darling.
Courage & other life answers you will find.

Seek comfort for your heart,
comfort for your soul,
and seek peace always.
Make it a goal.

Above all else,
Remember,
Always guard your heart.
Because out of it the issues of life flow.

You were born to win,
and fear is no longer in control.

Proverbs 3:24

When you lie down,
you will not be afraid,
When you lie down,
your sleep will be sweet.

Dedication

I dedicate this book to my mama, Ronnie. She read to me at night. She taught me the Lord's Prayer at 5 years old. She prayed for me as a baby. She helped to secure my safety in a cold world. Because of this I search the scriptures when I'm in need. She made sure I always had plenty of pencils and paper. She gave me my first set of watercolor paints. And here I am today fulfilling my purpose.

THE END

www.ingramcontent.com/pod-product-compliance
Lightning Source LLC
LaVergne TN
LVHW081454060526
838201LV00050BA/1799